For my friend Helen ◆ J. C.

For Tiziana ◆ J. B.-B.

Text copyright © 1996 by June Crebbin

Illustrations copyright © 1996 by John Bendall-Brunello

All rights reserved. First U.S. edition 1996

Library of Congress Cataloging-in-Publication Data

Crebbin, June.

Into the castle / June Crebbin ; illustrated by John Bendall-Brunello. — 1st ed.

Summary: Five friends journey to a castle to find out if there really is a monster living inside.

ISBN 1-56402-822-4 (alk. paper) [1. Castles — Fiction. 2. Monsters — Fiction. 3. Stories in rhyme.]

I. Bendall-Brunello, John, ill. II. Title.

PZ8.3.C8575In   1996

[E] — dc20   95-38197

2 4 6 8 10 9 7 5 3 1

Printed in Hong Kong

This book was typeset in Berkeley Old Style. The pictures were done in watercolor and pencil.

Candlewick Press, 2067 Massachusetts Avenue, Cambridge, Massachusetts 02140

INTO THE CASTLE

June Crebbin ◆ illustrated by John Bendall-Brunello

CANDLEWICK PRESS
CAMBRIDGE, MASSACHUSETTS

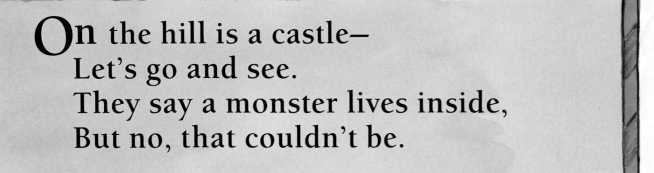

On the hill is a castle—
Let's go and see.
They say a monster lives inside,
But no, that couldn't be.

Around the castle is a moat,
Where slimy green things grow.
They say the monster swims in there,
But that was years ago.

Across the moat is a drawbridge
That creaks and groans, they say,
Because the monster stamps across—
But no one's here today.

Beyond the drawbridge is a yard
With a deep well built of stone.
They say the monster comes to drink,
But look—it's overgrown.

Across the yard is a passage
With a worn stone floor.
They say the monster made it worn,
But how can they be sure?

Along the passage are some steps,
Curving underground.
They say the monster thunders down,
But I can't hear a sound.

Down the steps is a heavy door
With a lock and an iron key.
I've never heard them speak of that,
So . . . open the door and see . . .

It's a dark, dank dungeon
With a bed and a wooden chair.
But who is sitting very still
In the shadows there?

Out the door

Up the steps

Along the passage

Across the yard

Over the drawbridge

Across the moat

Down the hill

And far away—

The monster won't catch us today!

But just a minute,
What's that shout?